APRIL'S RIDE WITH STONE

MUSTANG MOUNTAIN RIDERS

KACI ROSE

*To the Match of the Month supporters on Ream,
especially...*

Jackie Ziegler

*Thank you so much for your support. We couldn't do what
we love without you!*

*(To learn more about supporting the Mustang Mountain
Riders on Ream, visit https://reamstories.com/
matchofthemonthbooks)*

CHAPTER 1

STONE

HANDING Ruby my credit card to pay for the groceries I'm picking up, I listen to her as I catch up on the local gossip.

"You know I love the springtime in Mustang Mountain, but my Lord, your MC clears me out every year no matter how much I stock up," Ruby chuckles.

The first ride of the season is coming up in a week, so we have many of our friends from across the country coming to join us. It's a charity ride that helps support the women's shelter, but it's also popular because we go to Glacier National Park and ride the Going-to-the-Sun Road. It's become a favorite event.

This also means the clubhouse is packed with the other clubs, which bring tourism dollars to the shops downtown, including Ruby's Mercantile.

"What can I say, Ruby? Us MC guys can eat all day and still be hungry. We are built differently and have to keep up our manly bodies," I joke with her as I gather the last of my groceries for the week.

"Don't I know it?" she giggles.

As I'm paying for my groceries, I stare out the window behind the checkout counter, watching people pass by. That's when I see the one person I never expected to see walking down the street.

"What the hell? Ruby, if you'll bag those up for me, I'll be right back," I say, bolting out the front door.

Wanting to believe that I'm not seeing what I'm seeing, I walk out to the front of the mercantile. Sure enough, I see Howler walking down the street to the café.

Immediately, I pull out my phone and call Bear, my MC brother, who worked Howler over and sent him to jail after kidnapping Bear's girl.

"Hey man, what's up?" Bear answers the phone in an uncharacteristically cheerful mood. I hate that I'm about to cut that short.

"You took Howler to Sheriff Cade, and he was locked up, right?" I really need to know.

"Of course. When I left the jail, he was being processed. What's wrong?" Bear asks. His deadly serious enforcer voice fills the phone.

"I'm standing on the sidewalk in front of the mercantile, watching him walk into the cafe a free man," I tell him.

Bear lets out a string of curses. "There is no way he should be walking free."

"Agreed. Let me grab my stuff. I'm going to go talk to the sheriff and find out what's going on," I tell him.

"Keep me posted, and once you know something, you need to tell Atlas as well," he says, referring to our MC President.

"I will. I'll call you when I know something." Hanging up, I go back into the mercantile.

Ruby is holding my debit card in her hand and has my groceries bagged up. She can read everyone here in town like an open book.

"What's going on?" she asks, her playful tone from earlier gone.

"Someone from Savage Bones who should be in jail is out walking free. I'm heading to over to talk to the sheriff and find out what's going on. Do me a favor and stay vigilant. Maybe call Orville over to stay with you so you aren't alone, especially when you close up tonight," I say, referring to her husband, who also happens to be the mayor.

"Okay. Let me know what you find out and if I can do anything to help," she says. Most people would think she was strong and fearless. Knowing her the way I do, I can see the hint of worry on her face and hear it in her voice.

She's one of the few people outside the club and law enforcement who knows how bad Savage Bones has been getting lately. Mostly because it was her niece Emerson, who was kidnapped by them over Valentine's Day. She also happens to be Bear's girl.

Grabbing my stuff, I put it in the back of my truck and make my way to Sheriff Cade's house. John Cade and I grew up together, and he is one of my best friends outside of my brothers and the MC club. If he's going to tell anyone what's going on, it's going to be to me.

When I get to his house, I notice the police car is not in the driveway. Since he sometimes parks it around the back or in the garage, he might be home. So, I pull in, walk up to the door and knock.

Instead of John, his daughter Adaline answers the door.

"Hey, Stone," she says with a smile that makes my heart race. Then she steps aside, inviting me in.

I was there when this girl was born, but then I left Mustang Mountain to become a cop in the big city of Denver. I didn't like being tangled up by all the legalities involved when it came to helping people. Unfortunately, the cops were there to deal with a situation after it happened, not to prevent it from happening. I realized really quickly I wanted to be on the side to prevent crimes and bad things from happening. So, I left and came back home. But things here in Mustang Mountain have changed quite a bit, too.

The biggest surprise to me was that my best friend's daughter was no longer the girl I remembered when I left. At the time, she was a full-fledged teenager. I can't get my brain to reconcile that the woman in front of me is the same person. Now, she's all grown up and a woman that I can't get out of my head. She haunts my dreams and thoughts of her fill every moment of my free time. Though not another soul on earth knows that.

"Hey, Addy. Is your dad here?"

"No, he just left on a call. Dinner will be ready in a

minute. You'll join me, won't you? You know I hate eating alone."

John was always big about family dinners, especially after Addy's mom up and left them. John and Addy's mom were high school sweethearts, but she never wanted to be a mother. Addy was a complete surprise, and John convinced her mom they could be a great, happy family. That lasted just over a year.

When Addy was six months old, he proposed. She turned him down, signed over her parental rights, and left for L.A. to become an actress, saying that she could never settle in a small town. That was the last we saw of her, other than the few small roles she played on TV every once in a while.

So, Addy grew up with family dinners. Anytime I was in town, I would eat with them. It's not very often she has to eat by herself, and since I'm here right now there's no way I'm going to let her dine alone. An unfamiliar emotion tugs at my heart, and I'm going to take the opportunity to spend time with her.

"Yeah, I can stay," as I kick my boots off in the entryway.

The two of us spending time together alone is a dangerous game to play, but it's only dinner.

"Perfect. I just have to set the table, and we'll be ready to eat. I'll save a plate for my dad for when he gets home," she says.

I follow her into the kitchen. Whatever she's cooking smells mouth-watering. Addy took over the cooking role about the time she entered high school and got tired of the same old five meals that John knew how to prepare. Since then, she's become one of the best cooks that I know outside of my buddy Mack's wife, Lily, who is a caterer, and Bear, who is pretty damn good in the kitchen for being such a huge motherfucker.

I watch Addy as she grabs plates to set the table. But when she goes to grab the cups, she has trouble reaching them since they are on the back of the shelf and slightly out of her reach, even on her tippy toes.

She stretches, and the cotton shorts she is always wearing at the first sign of warmer weather ride up, revealing the bottom curve of her ass. Her shirt rises up too, showing a couple inches of skin on her stomach. All of her on display has my cock harder than it has a right to be.

"Being short sucks," she giggles. "Can you help me?"

When I stand up and walk over to her, she doesn't move to the side. In order to reach for the glasses, I have to crowd her in. As I'm pulling them down, my cock accidentally rubs over her ass. I swear she wiggles it against my cock. It's so brief that I'm not sure.

Had it been anyone else, I would assume they were flirting, but not Addy. There's no way this girl who is eighteen years younger than me has any interest in me other than as her father's best friend.

"Addy? Stone? I'm home. Everything okay?" John's voice calls from the front door and we shoot apart to opposite sides of the room.

Our eyes lock and I get a feeling we just crossed a line I had been holding myself back from.

I GLANCE at Addy before I look toward the doorway where my friend John will be entering. Addy's beautiful hazel eyes are wide, and she has no idea how to handle the situation that just happened. It's my fault, which means it's my job to take control and fix this to protect her.

"Hey John, I stopped by because I need to talk to you about something. Addy and I were catching up and talking in the kitchen while we waited for you. Since there are still a few minutes before dinner, can we pop into your office real quick?" I ask, throwing a wink over my shoulder at Addy as I exit the kitchen and meet John in the living room.

"Yeah, you know where it's at. I'll be there in a minute," he says, removing his jacket and gun belt.

I head to the office, sit down in the leather chair across from his desk, and wait. Moments later, he's in there with me, closing the door behind him.

"So, what's going on?" he asks, pouring both of us a glass of whiskey. Taking it from him, I nod my thanks, taking my first sip before I speak.

"Why is Howler out of jail?" I ask right to the point. John and I don't bullshit each other, as that was never our style.

I'm expecting some epic answer, but what I don't expect is for my friend to look so uncomfortable. He's tense, and the more I look at him, the more I realize that he doesn't look like he's been sleeping. He's lost weight, and also some of his hair. If I had to guess, maybe stress is eating at him.

"John, what's going on? You know you can trust me," I tell him, trying to get him to open up because suddenly, I'm worried that maybe he's sick and hasn't said anything.

"I didn't know," he says, and I swear his eyes get glassy.

Never have I seen this man cry, not even at his mother's funeral.

"What didn't you know? Whatever it is, we'll figure it out together," I tell him, trying to let him know that he's not alone in whatever is going on.

"That's just it. It's too late. When I was up in Whitefish, I went to a friend's bachelor party. What I didn't realize was that it was hosted by Savage Bones. They had some cards games going on, and I lost a lot of money, more money than I can hope to pay back. Even though I know they cheated, I can't prove it. Not that it would do any good. Been trying to keep them at bay, but they're demanding my loyalty, which is why Howler is out," he says.

Then it all starts to sink in. The sheriff is not on our side. My best friend is no longer acting in the best interest of Mustang Mountain. My heart sinks and my mind starts racing.

"Okay, well, let me talk to the guys. We will find a way to get you out of this." I know that the Riders and I can protect him.

"I'm in too deep now, but you need to protect Addy. Get her out of here, get her away from me, and keep her safe. I'm terrified they're going to go after her if they think for one second, I'm not completely on their side," he says begging me. He's pleading in such a broken way, in the way only a truly broken man can plead with the last ounce of hope he has.

"Have they threatened her?" I ask. His hesitation tells me I'm not going to like the answer.

"Not directly. Though it might have been indirect, there was no mistaking their threat. You are the only one that I trust with her. Please, please protect her. She can hate me all she wants, but I need her safe. You can hate me too, for that matter." He says the last part almost under his breath, but I hear every word.

I know he's already made up his mind. He's going to cooperate with the enemy, and he needs his daughter out of the way to do so. While I don't know what I would do in his situation, but the fact that he hasn't come to me for help pisses me off.

Furthermore, that a man of the law is giving in to

Savage Bones, knowing what they do, pisses me off. And that he doesn't trust me to help him makes me even angrier. Right now, it's taking everything in me not to let it boil over.

"Give me a day to get something set up and make sure that she's okay. Will she be fine until then?" I ask.

He nods. "I'll make sure of it. I'll tell her that I'm working on a dangerous case, which is true. You can tell her however much or little after that you want, or think is best."

The fucker was going to put it all on me to tell his daughter that he had flipped sides.

"Apologize to her that I'm not able to stay for dinner. Enjoy the last day with her and make your goodbye good. I will protect her from anyone who tries to hurt her. You included," I tell him as I stand up to leave without so much as a goodbye. I have plans to make because I'm going to make good on my promise to protect her from everyone... except me.

Addy

I'M JUST PULLING dinner out of the oven when the front door slams shut, and a moment later, my dad joins me in the kitchen with a sad smile.

"Is everything okay? I thought he was staying for dinner," I say, setting the food on the table.

"Something came up, sweet pea. He's not going to be able to stay."

I turn my back to my dad and open the refrigerator to hide my disappointment. Taking a deep breath, I turn around with a small smile on my face.

I can tell there's something more to what's going on based on the look on my dad's face as we sit down to eat.

"Dad, what's going on? I'm not a kid anymore," I have to remind him more and more lately.

"I know you're not, but that doesn't mean it's not my job to protect you."

"Dad, I..."

"No, listen. I'm working on a pretty dangerous case right now, and I can't talk about it. But I need you to go with Stone and let him protect you. It's not safe for you to be here or around me."

I can feel all the blood leave my face, and I feel like I'm about to pass out. One of the reasons I came home to Mustang Mountain after college was because of how safe it was. I hated living in a college town, in the city, not knowing my neighbors, sirens constantly, and all sorts of crime at my doorstep.

What kind of case could he be working in Mustang Mountain that is so high-risk? So dangerous that he has to send me to live with his best friend to protect me. His best friend who happens to be part of the Mustang Mountain Riders, and who are known for protecting the town.

"If it's not safe for me to be around, then it's not safe for you to be working this kind of a case. You're the only family I have left," I say as tears threaten to fall stinging my eyes and increasing the ache in my throat.

My dad squeezes his eyes shut, and I can see the torment all over his face.

"I know I am, baby, and you are the last bit of family I have left, which is why I'm going to protect you. But I also have a sworn duty to protect this town, and that's what I need to do. Sending you with Stone will keep you safe," he says, but the tone of his voice is off like he's not telling me something. I hate to think that my dad's lying to me, but if he is, it's for a good reason, right?

"Right now I have a few phone calls left to get things in order for you to be safe. I need you to pack a bag of everything that you will need for a while. I don't know how long this is going to take, but let's assume it's going to take weeks. But then I need you to go about your business as if everything is normal and do not tell anybody about this until Stone gets you out of here, do you promise?" he says, and fear starts creeping in.

"Daddy, you're scaring me," I tell him.

Instead of the soft and comforting face I am used to getting when I was scared as a child, his face is hard and almost mean.

"Fear will keep you alive. Please do as I say." He finishes his dinner and then heads to his office after setting the alarm on the house.

I've heard rumors about what's going on in Mustang Mountain. The mayor's niece being kidnapped, one of the Mustang Mountain Riders hits a girl with this truck.

What is going on around here?

CHAPTER 3
STONE

AS SOON AS I leave John's place, I head right to the clubhouse. We have other clubs starting to show up for the first charity ride of the season, which we do every year. Since they're staying at the clubhouse, it makes it impossible for me to bring Addy here, but also hard to talk to the guys.

So, I gather up Atlas, Thunder, Lightning, and Bear to update them in Atlas's office. Jensen and his wife, Courtney, who both run the women's shelter, will meet us as well. Once I get to the clubhouse, we all crowd into Atlas's office.

"Howler is out of jail. When I went and talked to Sheriff Cade, I discovered he let him out as a good-faith gesture to the Savage Bones," I tell them. Watching their faces, it's obvious that they're all surprised. I wasn't the only one blindsided by this.

"Why does he need to show good faith to the Savage Bones?" Atlas asks, irritation clear in his tone.

"Apparently, he was at a bachelor party for a buddy in Whitefish, and they got invited to some poker game. He lost a bunch of money and guess who was running the poker game."

"Savage Bones," the guys mumble.

I nod. "He didn't know that at the time, and he also knows that they cheated, though he can't prove it. Even if he can prove it, we all know that won't do him any good. But he owes them a lot of money, and he was basically playing both sides until recently, when they demanded his loyalty. So much so that they've started to make threats on his daughter, which is why he's now told me what's going on because he's asking me to protect Addy." I turn to Courtney.

"Which is where you come in. I'm hoping you have room at the women's shelter until I can figure something else out."

"Yeah, I have one more room available and it's hers," Courtney says.

I relax slightly, knowing she will be safe there.

"Fuck! A sweet girl like Addy? They would take her and sell her to the highest bidder without a second thought," Bear growls.

I know by the look on his face that he wants to hit something because I know the look very well.

"I'm not going to let that happen," I tell them, but Atlas catches my eye.

"You're right. We're not going to let that happen. You're not in this alone," he says, reminding me that they've got my back no matter what. Something that, even after all this time, still takes some getting used to.

I nod in agreement and make plans with Courtney to bring her to the women's shelter tomorrow. As I get ready to leave, I think about going home but second guess myself and circle back around going in a different direction.

I park down the street from John's house. I'm just going to sit there until I see all the lights go off and keep an eye on things, I tell myself. Then once the lights go off, I tell myself I'm going to stay for a little longer to make sure that nothing happens. Before I know it, the sun is starting to rise, and I still can't make myself leave.

It's impossible for me to leave Addy alone and vulnerable. Twenty-four hours ago, I would have said her father would give his own life to protect his daughter if the Savage Bones broke into his house. Now I'm not quite sure that would happen.

John steps out on the front porch and looks around like he's making sure everything is okay. When his eyes land on my truck, he knows what I'm doing here, because he nods in my direction, and then he goes back inside.

Starting up my truck, I turn around and head into town to grab some breakfast and coffee. First, I stop at the Mercantile and grab the duffel bag from the back of my truck.

"Stone, dare I even ask if everything's okay?" Ruby asks me when I walk through the door.

"Please don't ask any questions because I don't want

to lie to you. I really just need to use your shower upstairs." I hold up the duffle bag in my hand.

Ruby studies me for a moment, looking me over making sure I'm okay in that grandmotherly way she does.

"Of course, you know where everything is," she says.

Thankfully, she doesn't ask any questions, even though I can see them written all over her face.

This isn't the first time I've had to come in and use her shower or grab some food. We all appreciate Ruby's open-door policy to anyone who needs it. Usually very few questions are asked, which is remarkable because she just isn't the kind of no questions asked person.

By the time I come back downstairs from my shower, coffee and a bacon, egg, and cheese bagel are sitting on the counter for me.

"Bless you, Ruby," I say, putting a twenty-dollar bill down on the counter, knowing it more than covers the coffee and food. Then I'm right back out the door and straight back to John's house.

I'm not waiting any longer to get Addy out of there. The more she's around him, the more danger she is in. I knock on the door, and surprisingly, Addy answers it. She's in leggings and an oversized sweater with her hair pulled back in a messy bun, and she has no makeup on. Taking a minute to enjoy her girl next door vibe, I can feel my dick getting hard just from her standing in front me. Then I realize the danger she just put herself in.

Leaning in, I whisper in her ear, "Sweetheart, open that door again, especially since you had no idea who was on the other side, and I will take you over my knee and smack your ass red."

At my words, golden flecks shine in her wide eyes and she seemed to be holding her breath.

Even through the thick sweater, I can tell her nipples are hard points. Fuck, I didn't need to know talking like that turns her on. I only wanted to scare her, but knowing she needs a good spanking is something I will be fucking my fist to later.

"Sorry, Dad was just getting out of the shower. I didn't think."

I soften because this is all new to her. Stepping into the house, I close the door behind me as John comes into the living room. Without saying a word, I glare at him and stalk straight to his office. Silently, he follows behind me.

"Is she ready to go? Because I'm not leaving her here any longer. I've already got everything set up for her safety."

"She should be. I know she was packing last night. Where are you taking her?"

"Why the hell would I tell you? You are the whole reason she is in danger. If you know where she's at, the Savage Bones can use it against you to get it out of you. Once again, you'd be putting her in danger." I raise my voice because I didn't think he would ask that kind of a question.

"I would never betray her like that!" he says, jerking his head up to meet my eyes.

"Yet you already have. She's in danger because you

decided to work with Savage Bones, the fucking enemy! So, if anything happens to her, it is on your head. But I will make sure that nothing does and do the job that you failed to do in protecting her!" I'm yelling now, and I know it, getting out all the anger that boiled in me as I sat in my truck staring at the house last night.

Even though I know he's doing his best to protect her right now, she wouldn't need this kind of protection if he didn't put her in this situation.

"Is that true, Daddy?" Addy's trembling voice says from the doorway behind me.

"Fuck!" I say, realizing now that she probably heard every word.

I close my eyes and take a deep breath because this was not how I wanted her to find out.

John looks between me and his daughter. Then he stands and tries to take a step towards her. Instinctively, I get between the two of them. Looking at me with confusion on his face, he stops abruptly.

"Baby, let me explain..." He starts and tries to step around me, but I get back in his way.

"No! I... I can't believe you would do this," she says. Even with my back to her, I know there are tears in her eyes, and I want to punch John for putting them there.

"Stone, please get me out of here," she says.

With one last look at my former best friend, I turn, wrap an arm over her shoulders, and lead her to her bedroom to get her things.

"Is this too much? He said it could be weeks. Now, I

don't know if I'll be coming back at all." She says, clearly lost in her thoughts.

"Do you have everything that's important to you? If something was to happen and you were not able to come back for anything else, do you have everything that you would want?" I ask.

"Yes, the rest is just books and clothes," she says, looking around at the five duffle bags on her bed and the two large suitcases on the floor.

"I'll buy you more clothes and books," I tell her, and she looks up at me with a sad smile, but still so much hope in her captivating eyes.

CHAPTER 4
ADDY

"WHERE ARE WE GOING?" I ask once we are in his truck and away from my dad.

"I got you a room at the women's shelter for now." He says his eyes never leaving the road.

"Why the women's shelter?" I'm not sure why I can't just stay with him.

"Because they can protect you there. They have really tight security and everything that you need. Plus, I trust Jensen and Courtney to keep you safe."

"Let me get this straight. I get ripped from my home and placed in a shelter for something I didn't do. That sounds fair," I sigh, crossing my arms over my chest. I know I'm pouting like a kid, but this sucks.

Though I see a small bit of guilt cross his face before he schools his features again.

"Nothing about this is fair. I'm sorry. I can't tell you how much I wish things were different," he says, his voice barely above a whisper.

But I hear it loud and clear in the close confines of his truck.

On our way out of town, I watch the Mustang Mountains go by in a blur. Finally, he turns down some side roads and parks in front of what looks like in abandoned cabin.

"If that's the women's shelter, I think your idea of heightened security needs to be checked," I grumble, staring at the building that is boarded up windows and a roof that has seen better days.

"No, sweetheart. This is just the meeting spot. Very few people know the actual location of the women's shelter, and that's for everyone's safety," he says, smiling.

"Who are we meeting?" I'm looking around and right now, it's just us.

"The woman who runs the woman shelter married Jensen, one of my MC brothers, and he's supposed to meet us here."

No sooner does he finish telling me, when his phone rings.

"Speaking of," he says, answering, and then connecting it via the truck speakers.

"Hey Jensen, we're here waiting on you, man," Stone says.

"Well, that's why I'm calling. Last night, a woman with a kid showed up at the shelter and we had to give them the last room. So, unfortunately, we don't have a spot for Addy anymore. I'm really sorry, but these two look like they haven't eaten in weeks. We couldn't turn them down," the man on the other line says, sounding really broken up about it.

"No, don't worry about it. You take care of the mom and her kid. I'll figure this out," Stone says, hanging up.

"Shit, I can't take you to the clubhouse because in a few days we will have a bunch of different clubs visiting for our first ride of the season. They're all staying at the clubhouse. Even though they're good people, I wouldn't trust them around you," he says, staring out the windshield.

I don't bother telling him that I don't want to go to a clubhouse full of strange men, anyway.

"Just take me home. I know how to shoot. I'll be fine," I sigh. At this point, all I want to do is curl up with a good book and forget about my life for a few hours.

"Not happening, sweetheart. I guess I'm taking you home with me," he says. Then he puts the truck in drive, and we head to his home.

I've been to Stone's place a few times with my dad. It's a beautiful cabin in the middle of nowhere. When he built it, I swear he picked my brain having me describe my dream house. Then he set it on the perfect piece of land.

If his original plan was to take me to the women's shelter, it was probably because he didn't want me in his space. With me being there, it would put a cramp in his style. He wouldn't be able to bring home women.

The thought of Stone with anyone else breaks my heart and he isn't even mine. I have no claim on him, but my heart seems to think I do.

"I'm sorry you're stuck with me. Though I promise to try to stay as out of the way as much as I can," I say, leaning against the truck door.

While I get that he's trying to keep me safe, I hate feeling like a burden. Maybe this is my sign that Mustang Mountain isn't where I'm supposed to settle down. Since I have everything packed up already, maybe I should have him take me to the bus station. I'll buy a ticket and see where I end up.

Making rash decisions like that is not me, though. I won't be going anywhere without a plan, which means that I'm going to need to crash with Stone for at least a few days.

My mind is racing as the truck comes to a stop, but when I look, we're not in a driveway. We're on the side of the road.

"Look at me, sweetheart," Stone says once he puts the truck in park and faces my way.

Taking a deep breath before turning to face him, but I can't look him in the eye. Instead, I stare at the black T-shirt that he has on. He places a finger gently under my chin and tilts my head up until I have no choice but to look him in the eye.

"There is no need to stay out of the way because you will not be in the way. My house is your house while you are staying there, and you are free to be you. You will not be a burden. Having you there will be a blessing, so I'll not have to be alone all the time," he says, his eyes searching mine.

I have to wonder if I said the part about being a burden out loud.

"The only reason I didn't want to bring you to my house is because I have a lot of things like the First Ride going on. I'm not going to leave you there alone, which means you're going to have to let me figure out how to protect you. It would have been easy at the women's shelter, where there's 24/7 security. If you're staying with me, it just means a little more planning, that's all."

Believing every word that he said, I nod my head because I'm not sure what to say.

Stone studies my eyes for a moment more before he gets the truck moving again.

When we get to Stone's house, it looks exactly like I remember, even though it's been over a year since I've been here. The lawn is in immaculate shape, with the landscaping by the house ready for spring. The porch is decorated with a couple of rocking chairs and a porch swing ready to be enjoyed with the warm weather. By the shed to the side of the property, there are a few parked vehicles. When it's too cold to drive motorcycles, he keeps them in the shed.

After he grabs a couple of my duffel bags, he opens my door and offers me his hand to step out of the truck. When I take it, I attempt to ignore the sparks that travel through my body at the skin-to-skin contact as we make our way towards the front door.

Stone reaches around me and opens the door for me. Stepping in, I'm overwhelmed with how this cabin feels like home. It's bright and open and warm. And it smells like Stone. I'm not sure until this moment that I even knew he had a scent. It's pine and fresh, with hints of leather, and whatever aftershave he uses. I guess all along I've associated those scents with him.

"Come on, you can stay in the guest room. I haven't really done anything with it so feel free to decorate it however you want. Make it your space. I wish I could say that you're only going to be here for a short amount of time, but to be honest, I just don't know," he says.

I follow him down the hallway to a bedroom where he sets my duffel bags on the bed.

The room has a bed, a dresser, a nightstand, and nothing else. There are no sheets on the bed, no pictures on the walls, and there are not even curtains on the windows.

"Let me grab some sheets." He disappears down the hallway and comes back a moment later with sheets and blankets setting them on the bed.

"Go online and send me the link to curtains or whatever else you want while you're here. I'll get everything you pick out. The bathroom across the hall is all yours. My bedroom is at the end of the hall and my office is next to the bathroom." He stands in the doorway looking uncomfortable.

"Thank you," I say. Though I'm trying not to think about how close I'm going to be to his bedroom at night.

"I'm gonna go grab your other bags," he says, bolting out of the doorway.

With nothing else to do, I open my duffle bags that he's brought in and begin unpacking and putting them in the dresser. The room is plenty big and with a little decoration should be very comfortable.

"We can get you a desk to put over there in the corner." Stone says startling me, as he sets my other duffle bags on the bed as well.

"I don't really have a need for a desk, but I think that would be a great place to set up a reading nook."

"Let me know what you need, and I'll make it happen," he says with a soft smile on his face.

As the assistant librarian, I love books and spend a lot of my free time reading. All the time at work, I get asked for recommendations. So, the more books I read, the better, because then I can recommend them. Or that's what I tell myself, anyway.

"These are the last of the bags. I'm going to go make a few phone calls in my office. Why don't you go ahead and get settled and then we'll do lunch together?" Though he doesn't even wait for an answer as heads to his office, closing the door behind him.

I unpack my bags and with my stuff scattered around the room, it feels more like home. After making the bed, I sit down on it, gathering my thoughts.

It's hard to believe it's been less than twenty-four hours since my dad told me to pack a bag that I was no longer safe in my own home. Now I'm living with Stone in his cabin in the mountains. My life has been completely tossed upside down. But more importantly, right now, I need to stop myself from trying to picture Stone and me building a life in this cabin together.

He's being nice to me, but that doesn't mean he's into

me. Why would he be? He's so much older than I am. I'm sure he sees me as a little kid that he has to protect for his best friend. But maybe while I'm living here, I can use the opportunity to prove to him I'm all woman.

I don't want to live with regrets. Taking this shot with the man I've had a crush on for as long as I can remember is definitely something I would regret if I didn't at least try. If I embarrass myself completely, I can always buy that bus ticket and never have to worry about it again.

But what if he feels the same way...

"I AM NOT SITTING HERE in the cabin all day like some girl who's been grounded. Especially for something that I didn't do," Addy pouts after being told that she will not be joining me on the first ride of the season and that she is to stay in the cabin and not even go outside.

"You're not being punished..." I begin, but she interrupts me.

"It sure as hell seems like it, and I'm not going to put up with it. I'm not staying here, Stone. If you're not going to take me with you, then I'm going to go and hang out with friends in town at the cafe," she says, crossing her arms mutinously.

Hearing a cuss word out of her mouth has me fucking hard as hell.

She's already been here in my cabin for a few days. We had a nice routine going. She'd go to work, and I or one of my other MC brothers would keep an eye on her.

Then we would come home, have dinner, and she would read. Things were calm and quiet.

Now it's the weekend, and she's not willing to listen to me.

"It is not safe for you to go to a cafe and be out in public right now. All the guys are going to be at the First Ride. I have no one to sit with you." I'm hoping honesty will do the trick.

"Which is why I will not be here like a sitting duck because I guarantee you the Savage Bones knows that all of your guys are going to be out on the First Ride. If they're looking for me for whatever reason, this is the time that they're going to make a move. Even I know that," she says, lifting her chin and challenging me.

Fuck, I know she's right. I can't leave her here, but I don't know if she'd be much safer surrounded by rowdy members of the other clubs. I'm pacing up and down my living room, running through all the scenarios in my head.

There's no way I can ask one of the guys not to go on the first ride of the season. Because I'm the Sergeant at Arms I have to go, but at the same time, I can't leave her defenseless. Whether she stays in the cabin or goes into town, she is right. She'd be a sitting duck.

If she's with me, at least I can protect her, even if that means I have to knock the shit out of one of these other MC guys who is undoubtedly going to say the wrong thing.

"Fine, you can come with me, but you need to do

what I tell you. The other guys, we don't know all of them, so you stick by my side." I tell her firmly.

"Deal," she says with a smile, lighting up her pretty face.

All I can do as I go out to get my bike ready is shake my head and hope that this is the right decision.

She has the biggest smile on her face as we get on the bike and head to the clubhouse. Seeing that big, delighted grin on her face, makes me smile, too. Right now, in the midst of everything weighing us both down, I was able to give her this moment.

"Remember what I said," I tell her as I help her off the bike, and we go into the clubhouse.

If I can show some kind of ownership like she's mine, I figure the other guys won't mess with her, especially the guys from the other clubs. To make my point, I walk in holding her hand, making it abundantly clear that she's with me. The gesture doesn't go unnoticed by the guys there, especially the other Mustang Mountain Riders. Thankfully, they don't call me on it and just let it be, but I know I'll be answering questions later.

I take her back to the kitchen where there are some snacks for her. It doesn't hurt that she's also out of the main room and away from all the prying eyes of the other guys.

"There's a lot more people here than I thought," she says, nervously.

"The event grows every year. It used to be a small with one or two other neighboring clubs, but now we get clubs from as far as Texas and Maine joining us."

We don't have to wait long before Atlas calls everybody to get their stuff together and gives us the meeting point where we will gather at just outside Glacier National Park. We can't ride there in one big group, so each club is riding together to the meet-up spot. From there we will ride the Going To The Sun Road together.

"Last chance to back out, sweetheart," I tell her.

She just shakes her head. "Are you kidding? Getting to see Glacier National Park on the back of your bike? I am not going anywhere. Let's go, big guy," she says.

If I didn't know any better, I would swear she was flirting. This girl is going to be trouble. I can feel it deep in my bones. We head out, and I get her settled on my bike. As we get on the road and leave Mustang Mountain, heading north to the meeting spot, I ride with Bear towards the back of the group.

Addy wraps her arms around my waist and holds on tight. Her front is pressed against my back the entire way. Our group takes a more scenic route, avoiding the highways, so at one of the stoplights, I reach back and rub my hands up and down her legs on either side of me. I do it without thinking, but it's a move bikers usually only make with their old lady, though it feels natural with her. She squeezes me tighter and runs her hand up and down my chest. I bring my hands back to the bike handles, but I place one hand over hers, holding her hand above my heart. She doesn't know it, but she holds it in the palm of her hand.

By the time we meet the other guys at the meeting

location, I'm as hard as nails. Which is not easy to hide while riding a bike.

Atlas gives a speech thanking everyone for joining and then gives a brief talk about the charity that we will be donating the proceeds. Then he gives some safety instructions for the riders who are not used to the roads in this area.

We're going to drive down the road where there's a beautiful spot around the lake. It's tradition for us to stop for lunch there before driving back to the clubhouse. Everyone is welcome to go at their own speed and I volunteer to bring up the rear of our group. That way, the fewer witnesses to anything that happens between Addy and me the better.

Everyone heads out and we start the drive, taking it slow because the scenery is stunning. We're about half an hour into the ride when Addy gets my attention to stop at one of the pull offs. Suddenly worried that something's wrong, I pull over and shut off my bike.

"You okay?" I ask, taking off my helmet.

When she removes her helmet and shakes her hair loose, I'm riveted by her natural beauty. It stuns me so much that I'm speechless. With a big smile on face her face, she looks at the vista and turns to me. "Nothing. I wanted to get some photos here. It's absolutely stunning. I grew up in Mustang Mountain, but I've never been here and seen anything like this in my life," she says with awe.

After I help her off the bike, we walk along the overlook. She pulls her phone out and takes some photos before she looks back at me.

"Will you come take a picture with me?" She asks, shyly, like she thinks I'm going to say no.

Though I may not enjoy having my photo taken, if she wants a photo of us together, I'm going to do it. Walking over to where she is, I stand behind her, placing both of my hands on her hips and pull her back to my chest. We're facing my bike, and the view is behind us as she holds up her phone to take a selfie.

It takes a minute for her to get the angle right, and to get both of us in the photo along with the stunning background. She snaps a few photos, and without thinking, I simply turn my head to kiss her temple. It's captured forever in a selfie. Shit.

There's a sharp intake of breath from her and then she sinks back into my chest even closer than before.

At this point, there's no hiding how hard I am from her. She has to feel my hard cock pressing into her lower back.

"Stone?" she whispers, turning to face me.

My hands are still on her hips, and now her front is pressed against my front. My hard cock is pressed eagerly against her belly. Her eyes are running over my face, and I can feel each movement as if it was her hand gently caressing my face.

Her eyes land on my lips, and my eyes drop to hers. When her tongue darts out and wets her lips, I'm done. Right now, I couldn't hold back anymore if I tried.

I gently cup the back of her head and lean down slowly, giving her plenty of time to know what my intention is and to stop me if she wants. But she doesn't stop me and my lips land on hers.

The spark I feel at our lips touching makes my cock harder. I want to consume her with just this one kiss. She lets out a soft moan and wraps her arms around my neck, pulling me in closer.

Tracing my tongue along her lips, she opens for me, and our tongues meet. My legs nearly give out on me at just how perfect this all feels. I could get lost in her for hours and not need to come up for air. But the sound of a car pulling into the overlook grabs my attention. We're out in public, not in the privacy of my cabin, so I reluctantly pull away.

Not wanting this moment to end, I take a minute to look at her.

All because of me, her beautiful eyes are glazed, her cheeks are flushed, and her plump lips are swollen. She's never looked sexier or more desirable. When her eyes focus on me, a smile covers her face, and her hands cup my cheeks.

"Why did you stop?"

"A car just pulled in, and we're out in public where anyone could see you like this. Let's go catch up with the others," I tell her, even though it's the last thing I want to do.

What I want to do is turn the bike around and head straight home to the cabin, kiss her again and again and maybe even spend the rest of the day kissing her. But if we don't show up, our presence will be missed at the event, and Atlas would have my ass. So reluctantly, we get back on the bike and catch up with everyone else.

Soon enough, I'll have her all to myself. I should feel guilty about that, but I don't. All I feel is desire. I want to have her in my arms again.

TODAY IS the first event in a new series that I set up at the library, and it has to go well. This is my chance to prove to my boss that I can do this job when she retires.

Since I love all things travel, it made sense to pitch this idea of a travel series. Each month, we feature a new location and bring in books set in that location, both fiction and nonfiction. Then we try to get authors who wrote the books to come to the event where they would speak, sign, and sell their books, and answer questions. A win-win, we hope.

The head librarian, aka my boss, loved it. She put me in charge and today is the day. This month's location is Scotland, so the library provided a bunch of fictional books set in Scotland. The popular ones seem to do with Highlanders and time travel or historical Highlanders, but either way, it has brought in more interest to the library.

In preparation, we purchased several nonfiction books about Scotland because I anticipate they will be popular. Though we really scored when we got an actual Scottish gentleman to talk about Scotland and teach us how to make something for dessert called a 'Tipsy Laird'. And yes, to our delight, he wore a kilt.

"Are you ready to go? Thunder and Lightning are going to meet us there," Stone calls from the living room to where I'm in my bedroom, getting ready.

"Why are they going to meet us there? I didn't realize they had any interest in Scotland, and I've never seen the two of them pick up a book and read," I say, slipping on my necklace.

When I step out into the living room, Stone's eyes are immediately on me. Today the weather is a gorgeous Montana day, warm and sunny. So, I decided to wear one of my cute dresses along with my dressy sandals and my hair styled in a high ponytail. Since I'm the one putting on this event, I wanted to look stylish and put together.

"You look stunning. I didn't realize this was such a dressy event," he says, holding his arms up, showing off that he's in jeans, a t-shirt, and his leather jacket.

I take a moment to enjoy looking at him in the tight t-shirt with his muscular chest. It's drool worthy. He looks like what he is, a hot biker.

Answering him, I tell him, "It's not, but I figured since I'm in charge, I should look halfway decent. But you didn't answer my question."

We stand there for a moment, his eyes running over

my body, and there's a heat in them that he's not even trying to hide.

Our first and only kiss was just a few days ago, and ever since then, he's been more touchy-feely, but I can still feel him holding back.

"They will be there as protection. We're expecting a fairly large crowd, so I figured it would be best to have some extra hands-on decks. Besides, a few extra people at the event will make you look good to your boss."

Well, that's kind of sweet and kind of annoying. I don't know if I should be mad that he's turning this into such a big deal or let it go that he is trying to make me look good to my boss.

I decide to smile and just let it be as I don't want to cause any issues, nor do I don't want to be late.

When we leave, Stone helps me into his truck and the entire way into town to the library, I talk to fill the silence and to calm my nerves. I tell him all about this new series and a few of the speakers that I have lined up over the next few months. He asks me why I picked Scotland first and I tell him how much I love all things Scottish, and I can't wait to visit there someday.

He doesn't seem annoyed. Actually, he asks questions and pays attention to what I'm saying. Even my dad, at this point, would have asked me to be quiet until we got into town, but not Stone. He encourages me to talk and actually seems interested in what I have to say.

"You are so passionate about this that I don't think that it's going to be anything but a success, sweetheart," Stone says as we pull into the library.

His words shock me momentarily into silence for the first time this morning.

"Thank you. That really means a lot. I'm excited and nervous about this," I say as we head into the library.

While I get everything set up, Stone stays out of the way. First on my list is to make sure all our books set in Scotland are highlighted for those attending the event.

Since today is a teacher workday, the local schools are out so I'm hoping that lots of parents will bring their kids here. Even older kids who are interested will be welcome.

Next, I set up about around forty chairs in our event space, which would make this the biggest function we've had in years. Then I go and greet our guest author. Happily, I'm able to sit and talk with him for a while before everyone starts showing up.

Stone is in an intense conversation with Thunder and Lightning, who I learned are brothers. They keep glancing over at me, so I'm pretty sure they're talking about me. Every once in a while, Thunder or Lightning will break away from the little group and do a walk around the library.

I should be annoyed that he's so protective of me here in my own workspace, but instead I find it romantic. Maybe I'm reading the wrong romance books to find this a turn on, but nevertheless, it thrills me.

"I think we're going to need some more chairs," Thunder says as he walks back into my office.

"We never fill up the chairs. I'm not too worried about it," I shrug my shoulders, trying not to let how much I was hoping this will be a success.

"Well, the chairs that are there are already full and there's people standing around the room," he says.

Staring blankly at him, I try to process what exactly he just said.

Then, without a word, I stand and walk into the event space. Sure enough, the chairs are all taken. There are people standing along the wall and kids are sitting on the floor. All I can do is stare shocked at all the people.

Moms have brought their kids who would normally be in school today. We have all age ranges, even teenagers. Looking around, I see some adults, along with a group of older church ladies.

All I can do is stand there in complete disbelief. But only for a moment. Then my brain kicks in and I start asking the guys for help. They bring in chairs from the storage closet and help me get more food and drinks out.

Proving to be a problem solver, Stone places a call to Lily, a wife of one of his MC brothers. She's a caterer and has agreed to bring in more food because we definitely are going to need it before this is over.

"My goodness, I don't remember the last time I've seen it so busy in here," Ruby says as she walks in with her husband Orville, the mayor, at her side. It's not every day that the mayor attends an event at the local library.

"Yeah, you and me both! We were drastically under prepared for this kind of turnout," I tell her as I look around excitedly.

I'm excited that there are so many new people here I even ignore the fact that Priest, Bear, and Six are now standing around, too. But at least they brought their girlfriends with them as well. Even though I remember being introduced to hem at the First Ride, I don't quite remember their names.

The event seems to fly by. Fortunately, everyone is interested in what the speaker has to say, or maybe it's just his accent. I help him make the Tipsy Laird and we find out it's like a Scottish trifle made with whiskey. He thankfully thought ahead and brought several prepared ones, both with and without the whiskey, so everyone was able to get a little sample, and we all agreed it was really tasty.

He stayed quite a while, answering questions, and signing copies of his book. I am delighted that today we have had one of the highest rates at the library of people checking out books. All in all, it was a major success, and we even raised a good number of donations for the library. Another added bonus was that people seemed really interested in our future events coming up throughout the month.

Once everyone has filed out of the library, it starts to calm down, and the guys help with the cleanup. Before I know it, the event space doesn't look like it's had an event at all, thanks to them and their help.

After everyone leaves, Stone turns to me. "I've cleared it with your boss. You're getting out of work early. We're going to go home and change, and I am taking you out for a celebratory dinner at the Flathead Steakhouse. You deserve to celebrate after everything that you accomplished here today.

That steakhouse is the one by the ski resort, and fairly

expensive. Instantly, I have butterflies in my stomach. Even though he says it's just to celebrate, it feels like a date. While I don't want to push my luck, since we're right here in my office, but without giving it a second thought, I pull him in for a kiss. Because the only way that I really, truly want to celebrate is with another one of Stone's kisses.

He is shocked for a moment, but then his big hands go to my hips, and he pulls me in deepening the kiss. I can feel how hard he is, and I know he's attracted to me and wants this, but I can tell he's also fighting it.

When he grips my hips even tighter, the moan he lets out during our kiss gives me the courage to be bold and push him about what he's thinking.

Pulling back from the kiss, I ask, "So, is it a date tonight?" Though, suddenly my nerves take over again, but it's too late to pull the words back.

His eyes search my face like he's taking a moment to regather his thoughts after that kiss. I don't blame him. It seems to have scattered my brain waves as well.

"Do you want it to be?" he asks, intently studying my face.

Biting my lip, I nod my head because I want that more than anything.

His hands are still on my hips, and he hasn't put any space between us. For a very brief moment, he touches his lips to mine again and then speaks.

"Then Addy, I would be honored if you would accompany me on a date tonight," he whispers against my lips.

"Well, it took you long enough to finally ask. Let's go get ready." I take his hand in mine and practically pull him out the door.

The sound of his laughter follows us all the way to the truck.

I DON'T KNOW where bold Addy came from, but I really like her. I had wanted to ask her out on a date, but I chickened out and figured calling it a celebration dinner for a successful event would be easier. But she totally called me out on it. I've never been more grateful or turned on.

Because now this is an actual date, and I will be able to treat her like she deserves to be treated. Sitting here at our table in this upscale restaurant, I can't take my eyes off her.

Yes, I'm here with my best friend's daughter, with a woman almost young enough to be my daughter. I should feel guilty, and I do, but not enough to walk away. I fought this for so long I can't do it anymore. Come what may I'm going to enjoy the hell out of it.

She looks striking with her glossy brown hair styled with curls and her golden amber eyes alight with laughter. The dress looks great on her and shows off her curves, making me want to take her home right now.

For once, I even got dressed up just for her.

Even though this is not somewhere Savage Bones would hang out or even consider entering, I'm constantly scanning the restaurant.

"What looks good, sweetheart?" I ask as we both look over the menus.

She's biting her plump bottom lip, making me want to kiss her again. Finally, she names a chicken dish, and I find it on the menu. It's one of the cheapest items.

I know my Addy would rather have a steak over chicken any day, but I think the prices are causing her to double back and choose the cheaper dish. I'm not having that.

"Oh no, sweetheart, get the steak. I know you want it, and I brought you here for that reason," I tell her. At my words, she looks up at me with a question in her beautiful amber eyes.

"Don't look at the prices. Just get what you want. Money is not an issue. I would not have brought you here if it was," I tell her.

She smiles and looks down at the menu again, trying to hide the blush that covers her cheeks.

When the waitress comes back around, she orders the steak that I know she wants. I order a steak too and also an appetizer for the table.

I've had many first dates in my life, and most of them were absolutely horrible. I hate the talking and getting to know you stage. Most women on first dates ask the stupidest questions, such as your favorite color, what you do in your free time, and other things that are superficial and a waste of time to talk about.

But it's different with Addy. We already know each other pretty well, so the conversation flows. I know she likes her steak cooked medium, and she likes a loaded sweet potato over a loaded regular baked potato. I also know she's eyeing the chocolate cake for dessert, but won't order it herself, so I will be getting it for us.

She knows that I don't like the cucumbers in my salad, and will take them from me, so they don't go to waste. She also knows I switch to water after my first drink of the night and that I love the bread at the table with my dinner and not beforehand.

We actually have a lot more in common than I realized. I found out that she loved the first ride on the bike, and she is already asking when I will take her out again.

Every once in a while, I have a thought that she should have gone to the women's shelter. Because now that I know how she fits so perfectly into my life, it only cements the fact that I am not going to let her go.

My friendship with John is already out the window. If he's flipped sides, there's no bond or loyalty there. And I find that I don't care how mad he gets when he finds out that I've made his daughter mine.

All tonight's dinner did was make me fall in love with her even more. The way she smiles and looks at me, the way she giggles at my stories that I'm pretty sure are not even funny is priceless and makes me desire her with a vengeance.

Tonight, her fate was sealed, and she doesn't even know it.

When the waitress comes back and asks if we saved room for dessert, Addy says no, but I just smile.

"We will take a piece of the chocolate cake to share," I tell the waitress as she takes our dinner plates.

Addy looks at me her eyes wide.

Grinning, I tell her, "I know you wanted the cake, but I also know you wouldn't order it for yourself. You never do." I want her to get used to me spoiling her because it's going to happen more and more.

"My dad would always say I didn't need dessert. That if I wanted to find a husband, I couldn't order dessert on a date or they wouldn't be attracted to me," she says. Her smile is forced as she tries to pretend it doesn't bother her.

I'm starting to see a whole new side of my now ex friend and I am not liking it all. What other bullshit has he been telling this goddess about herself? How long has he been putting my sweet angel down? Well, no more. There's not going to be any more of that shit.

"Well, that's crap. You want the cake, you order the cake. I will be more offended if you don't. I had no idea he was feeding you bullshit lines like that, or I'd have put a stop to it sooner."

"He just wanted to make sure I didn't put on any more weight. I already have to shop in the plus size section, and I know guys like the skinny girls. I'm not blind." She nods to a table near us, where a guy with a dad bod is clearly on a date with a super skinny woman.

The woman looks like she hasn't eaten since high school, and you can see every notch of her spine in her backless dress.

"Now, you listen to me. That isn't attractive to me. I love those curves and I'd be completely okay if you put on a few more pounds because it gives me more to hold on to. Did you see the girls my MC brothers brought with them today? We love curves, baby. You don't even want to know what the thought of you pregnant with my baby does for me..." I trail off as my dick gets painfully hard. Fortunately, I'm saved when the waitress walks up to our table.

"Can you box that up for us? We need to get going," I say never taking my eyes off Addy. Once the waitress walks away, I drive my point home.

"At just the thought of you naked, I'm now hard as hell. I plan to take you home, strip off your clothes and show you how much I love every inch of you. Then I'm going to fuck that idea of you needing to lose weight right out of your head. If you don't want that, now is the time to say something and stop me." I tell her barely keeping it together.

She is staring at me wide-eyed. Her nipples are hard under her dress, and her breathing has picked up. She is turned on and I can't wait to find out how wet she is.

"I want that," she whispers.

Closing my eyes, I take a deep breath, and think about the abused horse case I helped Asher with last month. Hopefully, that will get my dick under control. When the waitress brings the cake in a box, and the check, I barely glance at it and toss down some cash with a hefty tip, and then practically drag Addy back out to my truck.

Once I get her in the truck and situated, then I get in and start it up to get the heat going before I glance over at her.

"Are you wet, sweetheart?" I ask needing to know if that talk affected her the same way it did me. She looks down at her hands in her lap, but when she nods, a beautiful blush covers her face. She is so shy, almost like a...

Then, a thought hits me.

"Sweetheart. Have you ever had sex before?" I ask straightforward and to the point.

"No," she whispers.

Fuck. She is a virgin, and now my dick is harder than ever. I shouldn't be excited that she hasn't been with anyone and that I get to be the one to claim her virginity. And while I shouldn't be thrilled that no other man has touched her before, I'm grateful that I'll be her first. Because fuck if I'm going to walk away and let anyone else have her.

"We can wait until you are ready..." I say, even as the words kill me. I don't ever want her to regret her first time, especially with me.

"I am ready. I want it to be with you. Longer than I should have. I've wanted it to be you..." She says, her eyes finally meet mine.

"Then let's go home," I say, focusing on driving us back to the cabin.

I can't look over at her, and I can't reach out to touch

her. Otherwise, her first time is going to be in my truck on the side of the road and I won't do that to her. If I'd known, I'd have made it even more special, candles and rose petals and shit. But right now, the least I can do is make sure it's at the cabin and she's warm and in a comfortable bed. *My bed.*

Just having her perfume filling my truck is making my dick leak and creating a mess in my pants. This girl is doing things to me no one else ever has, and she has no idea. She isn't even trying. All she's doing is just being her, and it's fucking everything.

The moment we get to the cabin, my truck lights illuminate the porch, and there is Hades lying there.

"He's here for his peanut butter balls," I tell her.

"His what?" "I made some peanut butter balls for him last year, and now he shows up once a week for his snack. I keep them on hand. Want to feed him?"

"Yes, please!" She says with the same enthusiasm as a kid in a candy store who was just told she could get anything she wanted.

Leaving her on the porch petting Hades, I go into the kitchen to grab a few of the peanut butter balls. When I get back to the porch, I hand a few to Addy who holds one out to him. Hades looks at me, then back at her.

"It's okay, boy," I tell him.

He looks at her again and more gently than I have ever seen him, he takes the peanut butter ball from her hand and scarfs it down. She holds out another and again he is so gentle, like he's afraid he's going to hurt her.

But when I hold mine out, he's back to his usual self,

drooling and coating my hand as he takes it from me, which makes Addy laugh. Hades looks between us again and then gives me a look almost like he can't believe we are together.

"Why don't you go in and get warm? I want you naked in my bed by the time I come inside," I tell her.

Once again, her eyes go wide at my dominant tone. Then she pets Hades one more time before disappearing inside.

"She's mine, boy, I can't believe it either," I tell him and hand him the last ball I brought out. "Things are about to get bad around here, boy," making him look up at me with more of a 'what the fuck' expression.

"The sheriff is helping Savage Bones. He's not on our side anymore. That is what started this and why Addy is here with me. But I have a feeling with him on their side, things are about to get worse. We could use any help we can get." I tell him while I scratch behind his ear in the way I know he likes.

He nods almost as if he understands me before he stands, runs off the porch and disappears into the tree line at the edge of my property.

Going inside, I take my time making sure the cabin is locked up tight because I plan to focus all my energy on my girl tonight.

CHAPTER 8
STONE

WHEN I WALK into my room, she is lying in the middle of my bed with the sheet over her. Even through the sheet, her nipples hard and pointing toward the ceiling. Her clothes are sitting on the chair by the wall, so I know she followed my instructions, which only makes me so hard my dick is pressed uncomfortably against my zipper.

After removing my shoes and socks, I slowly unbutton my shirt. Her eyes are riveted on me, and for a minute, I wonder what a sweet young girl like her could find attractive about a man like me who is so much older than her. Any doubts flee when I remove my shirt. The desire in her expressive eyes is hard to miss. Now that I know she likes what she sees, I send up a prayer of thanks that this woman was made for me.

Not wanting to rush this, I leave my pants on as a barrier. It's her first time and I'm going to make it good for her, even if it kills me. I want her to want sex with me, not dread it or think it's a chore.

Very slowly, I walk over to the bed and gently tug the sheet down.

"Don't ever hide from me. Your body turns me on more than you realize," I growl. As I take in her gorgeous curves, I grab my cock over my pants to show her how turned on I am.

"We didn't get dessert, but I want my dessert. Now spread your legs," I order. But the look of confusion on her face has me pausing.

"You and this sweet pussy are going to be my dessert. Have you ever had your pussy eaten before?" I ask, eagerly settling myself on the bed.

"No," she says, keeping her legs tightly closed.

Not deterred, I rub my hand up and down her legs and slowly pry them apart.

"The more of your firsts you give me, the fucking harder I get, sweetheart," I tell her, spreading her legs wide. She is already wet for me, and I can see it glistening on her perfect pussy. Settling between her thighs, I rest her legs over my shoulders, and take a deep breath, filling my lungs with her scent. Fuck, does she smell delicious.

I gently run my tongue over her slit, letting her get used to the new sensation. Her back arches, so I place a hand on her stomach to hold her in place and devour her. Every drop she has, I want. I circle her clit, and she is so damn responsive with her moans and gasps. When I suck on her clit, her hands tangle in my hair and she stiffens, crying out.

One moment she is pulling me to her. The next, she

is trying to push me away as the sensations overwhelm her.

I gently thrust a finger into her, and she cries out my name. She is so tight I wonder if just the act of getting my cock into her will split her in two. After a few gentle thrusts, she gets wetter, so I add a second finger and focus my tongue on her clit.

As gently as I can, I stretch her and get her ready for me. Once I feel her pussy flutter around me, I hook my finger and find the spot in her that makes her wild. Her thighs clamp around my head as her orgasm overtakes her. With her pussy gripping my fingers, I can't let myself think about what it will feel like to have her squeeze my cock like that, or I'm going to come in my pants.

As her body relaxes, I pull back and lick my fingers clean, but I can't seem to stop touching her. I want to feel her everywhere - her legs, her stomach, her waist. I haven't even gotten my hands or mouth on her tits yet.

"You still on that birth control your dad put you on before you went to college?" I ask because I really don't want to use a condom with her. I've never gone bareback in my life, but I want it with her more than anything.

"Yeah, it helped my periods," she says shyly.

"It's been well over a year since I've been with a woman, and I've been tested. I'm clean. Sweetheart, I've never gone without a condom, but right now, I want anything between us." I tell her, waiting for her permission.

"I don't want anything between us either," she says.

Not wasting a minute, I get rid of my pants and boxer

briefs faster than I ever have in my life. Her eyes go big as she gets her first look at the only cock she will ever have.

"It's all yours, sweetheart, and the only one you will ever experience."

When the meaning of what I just said sinks in, her eyes jump to mine.

Climbing into bed with her, I brace my weight on my arms, caging her in. "Wrap your legs around my waist, sweetheart," I whisper, leaning in to kiss her. It pleases me when she does as I ask. Then I let her taste herself on my mouth as I line my cock up at her entrance.

"I wish I could tell you this won't hurt, but I can't. What I can promise is to make it good for you," I tell her.

"I trust you, Stone," she says, wrapping her arms around my neck.

It's impossible to put into words what her trust means to me. I slowly push into her, enjoying her snug tightness. I've only gotten my tip in when she tenses, so I pause even though that's the last thing I want to do. In an attempt to think of anything but how wet and hot she feels, I stop, grinding my teeth with the effort. Distracting her, I lean in and kiss her soft lips. It's all I need, because she relaxes, and I slide in another inch before bumping up against her barrier. Deepening the kiss, I pull out before thrusting in and breaking through her virginity. She cries out into the kiss, but I hold still and let her body adjust to me. Then I glide my lips over her jaw and down her neck while I tell her how good she feels and how honored I am to be her first and how I'm going to be her only.

My words cause her to shiver, and she relaxes into me. It's then I pull back and thrust in again. My hard thickness fills her, invades her, making her moan. Finally, I'm in.

"How does it feel, sweetheart? You have all of me now," I whisper against her neck.

"It feels so good, Stone," she cries as I keep thrusting in and out of her.

"That's what I like to hear. Fuck, you are so sexy, baby," I moan as I wrap an arm under one of her legs and lift it higher to get a deeper angle.

She chants my name, and I can feel her walls flutter around me.

Keeping my pace slow and steady, I watch her face for any signs of discomfort. Her eyes are closed now, lost in the pleasure I'm giving her. I gently bite her neck, not hard enough to cause pain, but just enough to leave a mark. Her body jerks against me, and her walls tighten around me.

"That's it, baby. Clench around me. Show me how much you want me," I whisper in her ear, my hips picking up speed, driving deeper with each thrust.

Within moments, her body trembles, and she arches off the bed, crying out my name. I feel her inner muscles contract around me, milking me for every drop of plea-sure she can get.

My own climax building, I slow my pace, savoring the feel of her squeezing me tightly. I reach down between us and gently pinch her clit, eliciting a gasp from her lips.

"That's it, baby, come for me. Show me you're mine," I growl in her ear.

She does just that, trembling beneath me and pressing her nails into my back as it seems like wave after wave of pleasure crashes over her. Her inner walls clamp down on me once more, and I can't hold back any longer.

"Fuck, baby, I'm going to come," I groan, thrusting into her one last time before I let go, filling her completely with my cum.

"You are mine now, baby," I growl, nipping her jawline. "You belong to me."

Her eyes flutter open and meet mine, her lips forming a small smile. She nods, understanding the weight of the words I've spoken.

We lay there, panting and entwined, reveling in our shared passion. My cock slowly starts to soften, and I pull out of her, collapsing beside her on the bed. After I catch my breath, I get up, cleaning myself, and get a wet wash-cloth to clean Addy.

Then I pull her into my arms and cuddle her as we both catch our breath. I can feel the wheels turning in her head. But I let her work out whatever she is thinking about while I hold her and savor the feel of her curvy body pressed against mine.

After a bit, she still hasn't spoken, and I have to know what she's thinking about and has her so preoccupied.

"What is going on in that pretty little head of yours?" I ask, kissing the top of her head.

"Did... Did you mean what you said?" she asks.

Racking my brain, I think back through all the things I've said tonight.

"Which part, baby girl?" I ask, wanting to be crystal clear about what she is talking about.

"That I'm yours, and you are the only one I will ever have?" She says, ducking her head shyly.

I can't see her face, but I'm sure her cheeks are a beautiful shade of pink right now.

Before she knows what is happening, I flip her over and pin her to the bed, locking my eyes on hers. I want her to hear me, really hear me when I say this.

"I meant every word. I've been fighting what I feel for you for years, but now that I stopped fighting it, I'm not letting you go. You are mine, and I am yours. There is no 'till death do us part either because I will always take care of you. Not even death will stop me."

A brilliant smile lights up her face and I know she feels the same. Now it's time to show her with actions, not words. I'm going to make love to this girl all night long and love on every inch of her body. When I'm done, she'll know without any doubts how beautiful and precious she is.

CHAPTER 9
ADDY

THE EVENT the other day was such a success that I have work piled on my desk to go through. I don't want to stop, so I decide to eat lunch at my desk and try to get ahead of it.

Stone made this amazing corn chowder for dinner last night. When I had to work on the computer, he was very patient with me and didn't complain. The chowder was so good that I brought some leftovers for lunch.

Going into the little kitchenette that only the employees use, I grab the chowder from the microwave where I was warming it up. I get a creepy feeling that someone's watching me, but as I turn around, I'm the only one in the little break room. When I go back to my desk, the only person I run into is the head librarian. Since she's helping a customer, I don't take a minute to stop and talk to her.

Once I'm at my desk, I eat about half of the chowder because I'm starving, before I focus back on the forms on my computer. Even though my stomach starts to feel queasy, I eat some more of the soup, thinking that I shouldn't have waited so long to have lunch because now I'm not feeling so great. But I should feel better soon once the food starts doing its thing.

I answer an email, and before I can pull up the next one, I'm running to the bathroom, puking up my entire lunch into the toilet. Once my stomach settles, I flush the toilet, stand, and head to the sink to rinse out my mouth and wash my hands. That's when I see the note attached to the mirror.

Don't think we can't get to you just because you're hiding behind your boyfriend.

SB

Instantly I know that SB means Savage Bones. I take a picture of the letter, text it to Stone, and then finish washing my hands. Not a minute later, he's calling me.

"What the hell happened? Are you okay? I'm on my way down the mountain now," he says, all rushed, and I can hear his truck starting in the background.

"I was eating lunch and got sick. I ran into the bathroom, threw it all up, and saw that note. Right now, I have a slight headache, but otherwise, I think I'm okay." But my words don't seem to calm him down. He's at the library in record time, along with a few of his other MC buddies who are scouring the grounds for what I don't know.

"They're going to see if there's anything else to worry about. I'm taking you to the hospital," Stone says. Without another word, he ushers me out to his truck.

Here I was I was thinking that I would just go home and sleep it off. Yet seeing the worry in Stone's eyes, I'm not going to protest, and I'll go along with it if this will make him feel better.

As soon as we get to the emergency room, Stone takes control and talks to the nurse and the doctor. Before I know it, I'm back in a room bypassing the waiting room.

When the nurse leaves and tells us the doctor would be right in, I turn to Stone. "How did you get me ahead of all those people out there?"

"Well, the doctor has worked with us before and knows us. Also, poison is pretty serious. As soon as possible, they need to make sure they get it out of your system," he says as the doctor comes in.

Suddenly, there's a flurry of activity in my room. I'm hooked up to an IV, having my blood drawn and all sorts of tests are being done. Finally, they tell me that I'm going to need to stay overnight and transfer me up to a room on the third floor.

Once I get up to my own room, things seem to settle down. The doctor explains to us that the stuff in the IV is flushing my system, and I should eat as tolerated to make sure that I can hold food down. Stone listens to every single doctor's order to make sure that I obey them to even the smallest and most insignificant one.

"I'm getting sleepy. Will you come cuddle with me?"

I ask, after I finish the macaroni and cheese dinner that they gave me.

His face goes soft, and he nods as he toes off his shoes. I scoot to the side, making room for him. Getting into bed, he wraps his arms around me, holding me tight to his wonderfully muscled chest, and kisses my temple. With him enveloping me, I feel safe and comfortable and can relax.

Just as I'm just starting to drift off, I'm scared half to death when my father comes yelling into the room.

"What in the fuck is going on here? Stone, I asked you to protect her, not to fucking crawl into bed with my daughter. I can't believe that you're even in bed with her right now. Are you kidding me?" He's yelling one thing after another and neither Stone nor I can get a word in.

But I can tell the moment Stone's protective instincts kick in because he stands to his full height that is several inches taller than my father and takes a few steps towards him.

"What the hell are you even doing here?" Stone says crossing his arms and putting himself between me and my father.

"I had a call for someone who needed a ride to the hospital. When I got here, they told me my daughter was a patient. You couldn't even call me to give me a heads up?" my dad asks. Though, thankfully he seems a little bit calmer now, but not by much.

"Why would I call you when you're the reason that she's here? Savage Bones poisoned her. She's lucky the worst thing that happened was that she threw up her whole lunch, and she had to have her system flushed. All because of you. And you can bet your ass who ever told you she is here will lose their job. HIPPA and all," Stone says, and for the first time ever, I can hear how he got his name. His voice is cold and void of any emotion, yet scaringly threatening.

"You were supposed to be protecting her. Not... Not sleeping with her," my dad says, his voice shaky and his face completely pale.

"Funny, I could say the same thing about you. That *you* were supposed to be protecting her. But that's *my* job now. She's mine."

Stone and my father stare and lock eyes at each other.

Whoa! Stone just laid his claim on me to my father and I'm expecting my father to lose it. I knew we'd have to have this conversation, but I never expected it to be here like this over my hospital bed.

"My daughter? Really, Stone?" Dad asks, his voice sounding defeated.

"It's not like I planned it. All these years, I'd kept my distance for a reason. My plan was to take her to the women's shelter, but they were full. The only way I could protect her was by keeping her with me in my cabin. I didn't expect to fall in love with her, but I did. And honestly, right now, your opinion means nothing to me."

His words make it clear just like he did the night he took my virginity that I was his and he wasn't going to ask for permission for that.

That night when he took my virginity, I felt wanted. But here in the hospital room watching Stone go to toe-to-

toe with my dad, I feel even more wanted and cherished than I did that night.

Stone and my dad have been friends for as long as I can remember, and I know what my dad's doing right now is really shitty. But for Stone to put down and say that he doesn't care about my dad's opinion and walk away from that friendship for me? I should feel guilty about it, but all I feel is pride that this man is mine.

I'm surprised that the nurse who is peeking her head in didn't come sooner. She looks at both my dad, who is in full police uniform, and Stone, before looking at me.

"Listen, we can hear you two all the way down the hall. If you can't stay quiet you are going to have to leave, both of you," she warns.

"No! Stone stays here. Dad you should go," I say, and my dad looks at me for the first time during all this.

"I'm your father..." he starts.

Stone snorts. "That holds no weight after what you have done."

Then, looking at the nurse, Stone snarls, "She is over eighteen. There was no reason for the nurse downstairs to even inform him that she was here. If Addy wanted him to know, she would have called him."

At his words, the nurse walks over to me. "You didn't invite your father here?" She asks me softly, obviously intending for just me to hear.

"No. He should leave. Stone should stay." I tell her as she acts like she is checking my vitals on the machine next to me.

Turning to my father, she says sternly and adamantly,

"What the patient says goes. Sheriff Cade, I'm going to have to ask you to leave." Very few people tell my dad what to do. I see it so rarely I'm not sure what is going to happen next. My dad looks at the nurse, then at me before ignoring Stone.

"All right. I'm glad you're okay, Addy. I'm going, but call me if you need anything," Dad says.

"Don't bother. She won't. If she needs anything, she has me," Stone says, keeping himself between Dad and me.

Without looking at Stone, my father turns and leaves. Even though he's my dad, all I feel is relief once he's gone. Then I remember what Stone said to him.

"Did you really just tell my dad you love me before you said it to me?" I ask.

He stiffens and turns toward me.

"Yeah, I guess I did. That doesn't change how I feel. I love you, Addy. I would have told you the first time I kissed you if I didn't think it would have scared you away."

He walks over to me and takes my hand. The love he has for me is written all over his face.

"Addy, I would have told you that I love you before I told your father, but things have happened so fast. Because I do and have been crazy for you longer than I probably should have."

I marvel at my good fortune that Stone loves *me*. When I tell him that, the most beautiful crosses his handsome face.

He leans down to give me a passionate kiss that leaves

me breathless. Then, before he leaves the room, he says, "Good, because I meant it. You are mine and I'm not letting you go. I'd have just worked harder to make you fall in love with me."

I laugh because I don't doubt it for one minute.

TODAY, Addy is being released from the hospital. But she is to take it easy for a few days. We are heading home where she can rest, and I will make sure she does so. I can tell she is getting restless being stuck in the hospital bed, so I have a feeling she is going to give me trouble when it comes to resting for a few days.

Everyone has been in to see her, from her boss to Ruby and Orville and several of my MC brothers and their wives. Ever since her father left, Atlas has had at least one guy at her door, which was nice so I could get at least a restless sleep in.

None of that was enough of a distraction for all the thoughts circling in my head since her father's visit. His reaction is nothing short of what I expected from him, so I'm not sure why it hit me so hard.

I saw Ruby's judgment in her eyes when she visited. I see it in the nurses' faces, and I hear it in her doctor's tone when he talks to me. They all think this is wrong. My being with my best friend's daughter is darkening her reputation, and how can I allow that when all I want is to take care of her?

The problem is the women's shelter is still full, and if what happened at the library is any indication, she still needs protection. But I can only push her away so much. She will have to stay under my roof. Though she doesn't have to be in my bed, which is easier said than done because my cock doesn't like that idea at all.

One thing that I absolutely won't stop doing is protecting her with my life. Yesterday proved I let my guard down, and I won't allow that to happen again. I've already spoken to Atlas about having some of the guys help me watch her when she is at work.

She will be safe in my cabin, so that's not an issue. But the less time I spend around her in town during the day, the better.

Finally, the doctor comes in and goes over her chart one more time, giving her the okay to leave. The nurse follows, giving us our checkout paperwork. In order to make sure Addy will be taken care of, I pay attention to everything they say.

I help her get dressed and when they bring in the wheelchair, I help her into it as well. All the while in the back of my mind I keep hearing her father's words.

"Go get your vehicle, and we'll meet you at the front door," the nurse interrupts my thoughts.

Leaving Addy alone with the nurse doesn't feel right. My gut says not to, not after what just happened.

Thankfully, Thunder is here, and he realizes my hesitation, jumping right in.

"Hey, give me your keys. I'll go pull your truck around, and you bring her down to the door," he says.

I don't even hesitate and toss him my keys. Even though I don't let anyone drive my truck, if it comes down to my truck or Addy, I'll choose her every time.

The nurse walks down to the front door with us, and Thunder is there with my truck. After we load up, we give Thunder a ride to his truck before heading home. The ride is quiet, but every so often Addy looks over at me. Though she doesn't say anything and turns to look out the window like her life depended on it.

While I can tell there is something on her mind, and I'd love to know it is, it's best to keep my distance. Though I know I'm going to have to have a talk with her, maybe tonight, and I know she may not like it, but she'll understand.

Maybe.

I know she will.

She has to.

Once we get home, I help her into the house and set her bag from the hospital on her bed.

"Why don't you take a nap and get some rest? I'll figure out something to make for dinner."

"I'll lie down on the couch and read. But I've been doing nothing but sleeping, and I am not tired. Not at all," she snaps, picking up the book on the coffee table.

Nodding, I head into the kitchen and pull out what I need for dinner. I'm lost in my own thoughts as I make a recipe I've made more times than I can count: my home-made mac and cheese, which I know Addy loves.

When dinner is ready, we sit at the table and eat, and Addy fills the silence with how excited she is about all the new sign-ups at the library. She tells me about how she's already planning for next month's event and the huge boost in email sign-ups, too. Then she goes on about the good problem of having to work all the new donations into their budget.

Even though I wish that she shouldn't worry about work right now, it's obvious how excited she is and how much she loves what she does. This is more than just a job for her. It's her passion, and if thinking about it keeps her mind off of everything she's been through in the past couple of days, then all the better.

"Thank you for dinner, Stone. Let me clean up since you cooked," she says, standing with her plate.

I stop her. "The doctor said you need rest. Why don't you go sit down and pick out a movie and we'll watch it after I'm done cleaning up," I suggest.

Not that I'd let her clean up on a normal night, but not when she is supposed to be resting. Especially, right after being poisoned because I dropped the ball in protecting her.

She smiles agreeably and heads to the living room, while I take my time cleaning up the kitchen. Hopefully, she'll fall asleep partway through the movie, and then I can carry her to bed and go to my bed early.

Though my cock reminds me that it wasn't that long ago she was in my bed and that's where she belongs again. Certainly not in her own bed. Yeah, he's not happy at the possibility of her being so close, but not being able to have her.

I know, buddy. I want her too.

When I get to the living room, she has a movie pulled up and paused, with a determined look on her face. I sit down on the opposite end of the couch from her, and she watches me with a deep frown on her face.

"Go ahead and play the movie, sweetheart," I tell her, which, for some reason, seems to be the wrong thing to do.

Instead of playing the movie, she turns her body to face me. "What is going on here? You couldn't get any further away from me if you tried, and I don't just mean physically," she says, watching me closely.

I stare straight ahead, only glancing at her through my peripheral vision. "It's just better this way," I say, taking the coward's way out.

"Better for who? Certainly not me," she says, glaring at me.

"I saw the judgmental glares everyone gave me who came to visit you. Even Ruby, who would love to take credit for being part of setting up another couple," I tell her, still unable to look her in the eye.

"Ruby came over, gave me a hug, and whispered in my ear that it was about time I got you out of your shell and how happy she was for us. The glare that she gave you was because of all the distance between us and the fact that you refused to acknowledge us as a couple despite everyone already knowing that we were."

My brain thinks over Ruby's visit, and I start to see it with a new set of eyes. I was on the other side of the room, as far from her as I could get. I'm wondering if what she said is true, and I am so lost in my own head I miss her standing and walking over to me. She straddles my lap, wrapping her arms around my neck.

My cock doesn't seem to care that we're supposed to be putting distance from each other when her pussy is cradling it so lovingly. He's getting harder with every shift of her hips.

Attempting to hold her still, I place both hands on her hips.

"If you don't want me anymore, then you need to tell me. Don't take the coward's way out and try to tell me that this was for my own good, like I'm some little kid. After everything that you said? You said I was yours, and you said that you loved me. Remember when you said, and I quote, 'you are mine?' If you don't want me, have the balls to say it because I deserve at least that," she says, finally forcing me to look her in the eye.

The hurt and fear that I see there is my undoing. This girl is mine, and I love her with every part of me. At the same time, I know she deserves so much better.

"I love you, Stone. I'm not going anywhere. If you think you can put a wall back up, and try to walk away, you're sadly mistaken. Because I'm prepared to fight for us. Are you?"

Knowing she is all in, and that she isn't letting me take the easy way out, does something to me. How can I not be as honest as she is?

"Fuck, Addy. I love you, too. Why do I feel like I'm always trying to do what's right for you, and I fail? You deserve someone your own age who you can make a life with, not someone you're going to end up having to take care of. There are so many men much better than me."

"Why don't you stop trying to tell me what I deserve and what's good for me and let me decide? What I want and what I have always wanted is *you*. The whole age thing? I know that you're going to take care of me, so when and if the time comes, I'll be honored to be the one taking care of you. But that is so much further down the road that neither of us needs to worry about it. You are mine, Stone. And I am yours. Nothing and no one is going to change that. Do you understand me?"

Not only is she very serious, but passionate too. And her amber eyes are blazing with fire as she looks at me. I shouldn't find a turn on.

But there's something in the tone and in her words that makes me realize I need to stop getting in my own way. Once and for all, I need to stop letting my brain fight with my heart.

"Damn right you're mine, baby girl. Let me take you to bed and prove it," I tell her. Then I stand and she wraps her legs around my waist as I carry her to our bed.

Right now, this minute, I need to remind her as much as I need to remind myself that she's mine. There is no running away from this. And I wouldn't have it any other way.

CHAPTER 11

STONE

AS I PULL into Sheriff Cade's house, I do not feel the normal inviting feeling that I have felt with my former best friend over the last few decades.

Part of the dread that I feel is because Addy is not at my side. Not only is it not safe for her to be here, but this is a conversation I need to have with her father one-on-one, especially after his outburst in the hospital a few days ago.

So, I left her at the clubhouse with a few of the guys to protect her, including Bear, Priest, Thunder, Atlas, and a few of the other guys. Bear is cooking up a big lunch for everybody, and I know they will protect her as if she were one of their own. Simply 'cause she is mine.

Walking up to the front door, I ring the doorbell and wait. I know he's home. His truck and his police cruiser are in the driveway. When he opens the door, the shock of seeing me is on his face. He looks around, and I know he's looking for his daughter.

"She's not here. I left her with some of the MC guys to keep her safe. But you and I need to talk," I say, but not in the friendly tone that he's used to.

He nods and steps aside for me to enter.

"It's just me. We can sit here in the living room and talk," he says, pointing to the couch.

Instead of doing as he asked, I sit in the recliner facing the couch, so I have a direct view of him I speak.

"You might not like it or approve it, but Addy and I are together. She and I have talked, and this is something that both of us have been fighting for a while. We both decided that we're done fighting, and we don't care what anyone's opinion on it is because all that matters is the two of us."

Any softness on John's face disappears, and he glares at me. But I continue talking.

"I came here for your blessing to marry Addy. But I want to make it very clear I will be asking her to be my wife whether you give me your blessing or not. Because that blessing is for her, not for me."

His eyes go big, and he stares me down, almost like he's waiting for the punch line. As if I'm kidding that I'm ready to get married, and of all people, to his daughter.

He's always joked that I was going to be a bachelor for life, and I just kept saying I hadn't met the one, the one that turns my whole world upside down. I've told him time and time again that I would never settle, so he knows that if I'm going to marry her, how strong my feelings truly are.

"You think that this is something that she wants?" he asks.

I smile, remembering that night that we came home from the hospital, and I had tried to do the right thing and pull away, but she wasn't having it.

"Yeah, I've tried to push her away. I told her more times count than I can count that she deserves someone better. No matter how much I try, she won't let me pull away, nor will she let me walk away." All I can do is shake my head because I thank God for her. If I had actually walked away, I know it would have been the biggest regret of my life.

"It's going to take time for me to be okay with this, but I want my daughter to be happy. If you are what makes her happy, then yes, you have my blessing. That doesn't mean that I won't hurt you down and dismember you piece by piece if you ever hurt her," he says.

Despite everything that's going on right now, I do believe that he will protect her if I hurt her.

I can't be mad at him for wanting to protect her, because the more people that are on her side watching out for her, the better.

"Speaking of protecting her, what happened that made Savage Bones come after her?" I ask, getting into the bigger reason that I'm here.

He looks remorseful, which tells me right away he knows exactly why she ended up in the hospital.

"Wishful thinking, I know, but I thought if I could pay off the debt, this would be the end of it. Only they made it clear they don't want the money, they want my loyalty. Also, they told me that all this was done on purpose so I would not have an out. My friend who threw the bachelor party had no idea they were manipulating him and trapping me."

"So, what exactly happened to make them poison Addy?" I want to have as clear of a picture as possible.

"I offered to sign the house over to them. Then, I could cash out my retirement and pay the balance. They were not happy, and Addy was the victim of that one. After I left the hospital, I went right to them and pledged my loyalty." He looks down at his feet, and he won't even meet my eye.

"You didn't..." I say because I know clubs like Savage Bones sometimes require the guys to kill someone to prove their loyalty and give something for the club to hold over their heads.

"No, I made it clear that if I were to kill someone it would jeopardize them getting law enforcement in their back pocket. They decided to put their mark on me instead," he says. Lifting up his shirt, pulls down the side of his sweatpants, showing the Savage Bones logo on his right hip.

A message that he is stuck with them for life and there is no getting out.

"Fuck," I don't know what else to say other than he's totally screwed. How the hell do I tell Addy all this?

"This needs to be the last time you or Addy are around me. Don't come back to this house and don't bring her here. Take any of her stuff that you can with you today. Get married, be happy, but most of all, protect her," he says, tears glistening in his eyes.

We stare at each other for a minute, and I didn't know what else to say. Our friendship is clearly done.

"I will protect her with my life. But I need you to do your best to protect her, too. We will take Savage Bones down. If you're a part of them, that means you will be arrested as well."

He nods. "I hope you do. I never thought I'd be on the other side of a jail cell, but I would be happier if it meant that Savage Bones is no more and Addy is safe."

With that, I stand and head to Addy's room, where I pack up the books and clothes she left and a few odd things. It takes a few trips to the truck to load it up. When I'm in there packing up the last of it, John joins me.

"Listen, I've made some shitty choices, but I'm not a bad person. No one can know that you got this information from me. But Savage Bones is setting up meth houses all over on the edge of town. They are strategically placing them circling the town. Now that they have me in their back pocket, their plan is for me to turn a blind eye to it."

"We knew whatever they were getting into wasn't going to be good. Thank you for telling me, and I will prepare the others," I say, grabbing the last of Addy's things and saying nothing more as I head out the door.

We always knew Savage Bones was into some really bad shit. But knowing that they're closing in on Mustang Mountain because they now have the sheriff in their back pocket means we are running out of time.

I need to talk to Atlas and see what he wants to do.

First, I need to go into town and talk to Ruby because I can't wait much longer to make sure that Addy is tied to me in every possible way.

There's no safer place for her to be than my wife.

CHAPTER 12

ADDY

"DO you mind if we make a stop on the way home?" Stone asks me after he picks me up from the clubhouse.

He seems nervous about something, but I don't want to push, at least not right now.

"You know I don't care," I tell him, reaching for his hand. "What did you have to talk to my dad about?"

He glances over at me before his eyes are back on the road.

"How did you know I was talking to your dad?"

"Well, the boxes of my things in the back kind of gave it away," I tease him.

He frowns, but just shakes his head.

"After the hospital, I wanted to clear the air. Since I was there, I grabbed the last of your stuff."

I've known Stone for a long time, and he has little tells, just like I'm sure I do. That's how I know he's not giving me the full truth.

"And..." I tried to coax it out of him, but he looks at me with the same frown on his face.

"Stone, I've known you a long time. The dating part might be new, but you've had dinner so many times with me and my dad, I can tell when you're leaving something out."

"Sometimes there are things I don't want to tell you because I want to protect you. Sometimes, there will be things, no matter how much you try to pull them out of me, that I will not tell you because keeping you safe, sane, and happy will always come first."

"And is this one of those times? Because this is my father, we're talking about. I know he's in trouble. I know it's not the kind of trouble I can help him with. I also know that whatever happened with me being poisoned had to do with him." I tell him honestly.

"It did. Your dad was still trying to find a way out of his situation, and Savage Bones was not having it. You were just an expendable piece, and they used it to force your dad's hand in pledging fealty to them."

"What does that mean?" I ask.

"It means that to protect you, he pledged to Savage Bones. They marked him permanently. So, when the Mustang Mountain Riders take Savage Bones down and dismantle them, your dad will end up behind bars. He knows that, and he's ready for it." Stone says defeat clear in his voice.

Biting my lip, I look out the window as I let what Stone said sink in. Once we turn onto Main Street, I glance over at him.

"I haven't spent a lot of time thinking about what my dad did and what it means, but I guess in the back of my head, I've always known that he was going to serve jail time for this. Even if there was no us, going back to him wouldn't be an option either."

"Enough with the heavy stuff, sweetheart. We can talk about this some other day," Stone says, switching the subject as he pulls into City Park on the north end of Main Street.

The sun is starting to set, and we seem to be the only ones there. Once we park in the lot, the walkway is lit up with little paper lanterns. I don't remember there being any event at the park today, but Stone leads me down the path following the lanterns to one of the fields where they open up into the shape of a big heart.

I freeze in my tracks, but Stone keeps walking to the center of the heart before turning and looking at me. Even though I open my mouth to ask what's going on, no words come out.

But before I can speak, he drops down to one knee in front of me. My knees get wobbly, but I force myself to take a few steps towards him as he reaches into his pocket and pulls out a black velvet box.

When he opens the box, a shimmering diamond ring catches the last golden rays of the sun setting behind him. Stone's eyes are locked with mine, his expression a mix of nervousness and determination.

"Addy, I know things have been complicated, and we've been through more than most couples ever do in a lifetime. But through it all, I've realized that you are my constant, my rock, my home. Will you do me the honor of becoming my wife?" he asks, his voice wavering slightly with emotion.

Tears are pricking at the corners of my eyes as I look down at him, the man who has stood by me through thick and thin, who has always put my safety and happiness above all else. Without any hesitation, I nod vigorously, unable to find words through the overwhelming rush of emotions.

Stone's face breaks into a relieved smile as he slips the dazzling ring onto my finger.

He stands, his dark chocolatey eyes are lit with a fire, and they never leave mine. "I love you, Addy," he whispers, his voice filled with raw emotion. "I promise to always protect you, to stand by you no matter what challenges come our way."

Wrapping my arms around him, I hold onto him as if he might disappear if I let go. The weight of his words settles deep within me, anchoring me to this moment of pure perfection.

"I love you too, Stone," I reply softly, feeling the warmth of his hand in mine. "And I believe in us. And I agree. No matter what challenges come our way, we'll face them together."

MUSTANG MOUNTAIN HAS BEEN through a lot in the past few months, but the hits just kept coming. I looked around the room at my fellow Mustang Mountain Riders. We'd gathered this afternoon so Atlas, the MC President, and I could update everyone on what the hell had been going on.

Atlas stepped into the room and headed toward me. "You ready to get started?"

"Just say the word." He looked tired. We'd all been burning the candle at both ends and in the middle trying to stay a few steps ahead of the Savage Bones.

"Let's go."

I pushed off from the bar and followed him into the conference room where we conducted club business. A few of the guys had already taken their spots around the huge table. I nodded at Jackson and Dean, then stopped to shake hands with Six and Bear as I rounded the table and took my spot next to Atlas.

The rest of the guys filtered into the room. Conversations came to an end and smiles were replaced with furrowed brows and frowns. My game face slid into place. That's what my brother Lightning used to call it when I gritted my teeth and got myself psyched up for battle. Back then, I waged war in football stadiums and left the fight on the field. Now the battle was taking place way too close to home. It was time to put an end to the opposition.

Atlas started by summarizing everything that had been happening around Mustang Mountain since the first of the year. From Six coming across a woman fleeing the Savage Bones through the woods on New Year's Day to Stone finding out Sheriff Cade had turned and was now working against us, we'd been up to our armpits in trying to protect our town from those bastards.

"Thunder, you want to tell them the plan?" Atlas leaned back in his chair as he turned the floor over to me. As the Vice President of the club, he'd asked me to come up with a strategy that would shut them down for good.

I was used to rallying my teammates and getting them hyped up before a big game. Being part of an MC wasn't much different than being part of a professional sports team except I'd never had to look my teammates in the eye and know they were actually putting their lives on the line.

"We're all aware of the tactics Savage Bones is using to try to take over our town. They play dirty and don't have the same respect for the land or the lives of the people who make Mustang Mountain their home." I scanned the faces of my MC brothers. A few of them had already been injured while fending off the Savage Bones. "When you joined this club, you swore an oath to protect our mountain. None of us expected that would mean risking our lives."

A couple of guys nodded. Though we put ourselves in danger when it came to helping with the women's shelter or occasionally teaching some lowlife to pick on someone his own size, we were a relatively peaceful bunch.

"If any of you feel like you're in over your heads, now's the time to speak up. You can turn in your cut and be free to go." I paused, waiting to see if anyone would take us up on the offer.

Atlas had confided that he expected at least one or two of our older members to walk away. I disagreed. All of us had something to lose if the Savage Bones took control. The men in our MC weren't the type to start a fight, but they also weren't the type to walk away when one landed on their doorstep.

"No one's leaving, brother." Priest pounded his fist on the table then held it to his heart. "I'll defend my home and all of yours,"—Priest looked around the table and made brief eye contact with each of the men—"until my dying breath."

"To Mustang Mountain," a chorus of voices chanted. Everyone copied Priest and beat their fists against their chest.

I offered Atlas a knowing grin. "Looks like we're all committed to seeing this through. The sheriff's office has been compromised, so we're on our own. We'll use the clubhouse as headquarters, and I'm going to need a few men posted here around the clock. The rest of you will take shifts. I've broken the area into ten different zones, and we'll need at least one man on patrol in each zone at all times. Thanks to Stone we know the Savage Bones have been trying to set up some meth houses in the area. If you see anything suspicious, let one of the officers know and we'll get a team to check it out."

The men listened while I outlined the rest of the plan. Anyone with family was encouraged to move them onto clubhouse property where they would be secure. There were still a few weeks before summer vacation, so we'd have a guy posted at each school in the area during the day.

I made sure to put myself on the schedule for a daytime shift downtown. That would let me keep an eye on the curvy blonde I hadn't been able to get out of my head for the past couple of months. Ashley had been roommates with Priest's girl Rae before he locked that relationship down. I knew better than to get involved with a woman half my age, but it hadn't stopped me from checking in on her at the café where she served lunch most days. The meatloaf was good, but it was her smile that kept me coming back.

"Sounds like you've got everything under control." Atlas pushed back from the table and stood.

I was about to tell him we were only getting started when the door to the conference room flew open.

Ashley stood in the open doorway, her eyes wide. "I need help."

My heart catapulted into my throat as I covered the distance between us in a few long strides. Her hands were stained with blood. My gaze scanned over her, trying to figure out where she'd been injured. If those bastards had touched a single hair on her gorgeous head, they'd have to deal with me.

NEED MORE STONE AND ADDY? **Sign up for our newsletter** and get the free bonus scene here: https://www.matchofthemonthbooks.com/Stone-Bonus

Join Match of the Month Books on REAM to get an exclusive bonus scene, plus early access to other Match of the Month books, signed paperbacks, and more!

Next up, pre-order May's Ride with Thunder here: https://www.matchofthemonthbooks.com/May-Thunder

OTHER MATCH OF THE MONTH BOOKS

Mountain Men of Mustang Mountain Series

Welcome to Mustang Mountain where love runs as wild as the free-spirited horses who roam the hillsides. Framed by rivers, lakes, and breathtaking mountains, it's also the place the Mountain Men of Mustang Mountain call home. They might be rugged and reclusive, but they'll risk their hearts for the curvy girls they love.

January is for Jackson - Jackson & Emma
February is for Ford - Ford & Luna
March is for Miles - Miles & Kinley
April is for Asher - Asher & Jenna
May is for Mack - Mack & Lily
June is for Jensen - Jensen & Courtney
July is for Jonas - Jonas & Madeline
August is for Ace - Ace & Everly

September is for Shaw - Shaw & Eden
October is for Owen - Owen & Kennedy
November is for Nate - Nate & Ainsley
December is for Dean - Dean & Holly

Mustang Mountain Riders Series

Welcome to Mustang Mountain, where engines roar and loyalty reigns supreme. Beneath the shadowy peaks of the mountain, the Mustang Mountain Riders defend their ground against a dangerous gang trying to take over their small town. Forged in fire and steel, these bikers face threats head-on, riding hard and fighting even harder. While they brave countless battles, nothing prepares them for love sparked by the curvy women who steal their hearts.

January's Ride with Six - Six & Ginger
February's Ride with Bear - Bear & Emerson
March's Ride with Priest - Priest & Rae
April's Ride with Stone - Stone & Adaline
May's Ride with Thunder - Thunder & Ashley
June's Ride with Lightning - Lightning & Piper
July's Ride with Juice - Juice & Sammy
August's Ride with Arrow - Arrow & Katherine
September's Ride with Crank - Crank & Poppy
October's Ride with Atlas - Atlas & Bex
November's Ride with Viper - Viper & Marlowe
December's Ride with Scar - Scar & Evelyn

To learn more about Mustang Mountain...

- Visit our website:
(https://www.matchofthemonthbooks.com/)

- Join our newsletter here:
(http://subscribepage.io/MatchOfTheMonth)

- Follow us on REAM here:
(https://reamstories.com/matchofthemonthbooks)

ACKNOWLEDGMENTS

A huge, heartfelt thanks goes to everyone who's supported us in our writing, especially our HUSSIES of Mountain Men of Mustang Mountain supporters:

Jackie Ziegler

To learn more about the Mountain Men of Mustang Mountain on REAM, visit us here: https://reamstories. com/matchofthemonthbooks.

OTHER BOOKS BY KACI ROSE

Oakside Military Heroes Series

Saving Noah – Lexi and Noah

Saving Easton – Easton and Paisley

Saving Teddy – Teddy and Mia

Saving Levi – Levi and Mandy

Saving Gavin   Gavin and Lauren

Saving Logan – Logan and Faith

Saving Ethan – Bri and Ethan

Saving Zane – Zane

Mountain Men of Whiskey River

Take Me To The River – Axel and Emelie

Take Me To The Cabin – Phoenix and Jenna

Take Me To The Lake – Cash and Hope

Taken by The Mountain Man - Cole and Jana

Take Me To The Mountain – Bennett and Willow

Take Me To The Edge – Storm and River

Mountain Men of Mustang Mountain

February is for Ford – Ford and Luna

April is for Asher – Asher and Jenna

June is for Jensen - Jensen and Courtney

August is for Ace - Ace and Everly

October is for Owen - Owen and Kennedy

December is for Dean - Dean and Holly

Club Red – Short Stories

Daddy's Dare – Knox and Summer

Sold to my Ex's Dad - Evan and Jana

Jingling His Bells – Zion and Emma

Club Red: Chicago

Elusive Dom

Forbidden Dom

Chasing the Sun Duet

Sunrise – Kade and Lin

Sunset – Jasper and Brynn

Rock Stars of Nashville

She's Still The One – Dallas and Austin

Standalone Books

Texting Titan - Denver and Avery

Accidental Sugar Daddy – Owen and Ellie

Stay With Me Now – David and Ivy

Midnight Rose - Ruby and Orlando

Committed Cowboy – Whiskey Run Cowboys

Stalking His Obsession - Dakota and Grant

Falling in Love on Route 66 - Weston and Rory

Billionaire's Marigold - Mari and Dalton

A Baby for Her Best Friend – Nick and Summer

CONNECT WITH KACI ROSE

Website
Facebook
Kaci Rose Reader's Facebook Group
TikTok
Instagram
Twitter
Goodreads
Book Bub
Join Kaci Rose's VIP List (Newsletter)

ABOUT KACI ROSE

Kaci Rose writes steamy contemporary romances mostly set in small towns. She grew up in Florida but now lives in a cabin in the mountains of East Tennessee.

She is a mom to 5 kids, a rescue dog who is scared of his own shadow, an energetic young German Shepard who is still in training, a sleepy old hound who adopted her, and a reluctant indoor cat.

Kaci loves to travel, and her goal is to visit all 50 states before she turns 50. She has 17 more to go, mostly in the Midwest and on the West Coast!

She also writes steamy cowboy romances as Kaci M. Rose.

PLEASE LEAVE A REVIEW!

I love to hear from my readers! Please **head over to your favorite store and leave a review** of what you thought of this book!